BEATRICE BLY'S RULES FOR SPIES

MYSTERY GOO

Sue Fliess · Illustrated by Beth Mills

PIXEL+INK

To Christine, for getting me out of sticky situations since 1973. —SF

For my little spies Archer, Margot, and their upcoming little brother. —B.M.

PIXEL+INK

Text copyright © 2022 by Sue Fliess
Illustrations copyright © 2022 by Bethany Mills
All rights reserved
Pixel+Ink is a division of TGM Development Corp.
Printed and bound in December 2021 at C&C Offset, Shenzhen, China
Cover and interior design by Georgia Morrissey
www.pixelandinkbooks.com
Library of Congress Cataloging in Publication Data
Names: Fliess, Sue, author. | Mills, Beth, 1986- illustrator.
Title: Mystery goo / Sue Fliess ; illustrated by Beth Mills.
Description: First edition. | New York : Pixel+Ink, [2022] | Series:
Beatrice Bly's rules for spies | Audience: Ages 4-7. | Audience: Grades 2-3. |
Summary: When a gooey mystery shows up on her desk, spy-in-training Beatrice Bly and her best friend
use their sleuthing skills to solve a sticky mystery and find the perfect science fair project.
Identifiers: LCCN 2021034953 | ISBN 9781645950615 (hardcover) | ISBN 9781645950981 (ebook)
Subjects: CYAC: Spies—Fiction. | Science projects—Fiction. | Mystery and
detective stories. | Friendship—Fiction. | LCGFT: Picture books.
Classification: LCC PZ7.F63935 My 2022 | DDC [E]—dc23
LC record available at https://lccn.loc.gov/2021034953
ISBN 978-1-64595-061-5
eBook ISBN 978-1-64595-098-1
First Edition
1 3 5 7 9 10 8 6 4 2

Beatrice Bly's first spy mission had been a success. She was feeling confident. And restless. Because any good spy knows there is always another mission brewing.

She added to her list of rules:

SUPER SPY RULES

* Expect the unexpected

* Exercise regularly (Spies are always on the move)

* Have a Backup Plan (Spy work is unpredictable!)

One morning at school, Miss Leland made an announcement. "Okay, students, it's time to choose partners and projects for the upcoming science fair."

"More like science *un*fair," muttered Beatrice. "This is going to cut into my spying time."

"Fair or not," said Nora, "we have a project to do. Right, partner?"

"Right," grumbled Beatrice.

"If you've already chosen a partner," said Miss Leland, "raise your hand."

Beatrice started to lift her arm, but it stuck to the table.

"Ew," she said. "Sticky."

"Maybe something spilled," said Nora.

"Probably by a messy kid. But why *this* table?"

"Coincidence?"

"There are no coincidences." Beatrice pulled out her magnifying glass and inspected the spot. "Someone is behind this."

"Maybe it's just a sticky table," said Nora.

"*Maybe* it's my new mission," whispered Beatrice. "Collect a sample."

"Here we go again." Nora sighed, then scraped the goo off the table and into a snack container.

At snack time, Beatrice and Nora watched for messy classmates and thought of sticky substances.

"Lucy's lunch bag leaks," said Nora.

"Spencer brings fruit gummies," added Beatrice.

"Could it be glue?" suggested Nora.

"Or hand sanitizer!" said Beatrice.

Beatrice got out her notebook and the pair wrote down goo possibilities:

gummies

juice

glue

hand sanitizer

"We'll need samples," said Beatrice.

"Class, please clean up," Miss Leland said.

"Then follow me outside for recess."

Beatrice and Nora waited.

When the last student left the classroom, Beatrice tiptoed to the trash can and used her Grabbit3000 to pluck the evidence from the bin.

"Did you get it?" asked Nora.

"Affirmative. And Spencer's wrapper still had a gummy stuck to the bottom!"

On their way to recess, Nora popped into the art room for glue.

Beatrice opened the janitor's closet and borrowed a bottle of hand sanitizer.

"We can look at them under my microscope tonight and compare them to the goo," Nora suggested.

That evening, Beatrice and Nora examined bits of each sticky sample.

"I think I see sugar molecules in the goo," said Nora.

"The hand sanitizer has tiny circles," said Beatrice when it was her turn. "It's runny, though, not sticky."

"And Lucy's juice is purple, not gold like the goo."

They looked at the gummy.

"Ugh," said Nora. "It's too solid. Not gooey enough. Well, we tried."

Beatrice sniffed the goo. "Smells sweet. I have an idea."

"For the science fair?" asked Nora.

"For the Backup Plan."

"I think it's time to abandon the mission," said Nora.

"Good spies never leave a mission unfinished."

"But it seems we're not getting anywhere."

"Nora, not everything is what it seems."

The next day, Beatrice said, "My spy hunch tells me we missed something. Maybe the goo was *already* inside the classroom. Let's check again."

Nora crossed her arms. "Nope."

"I *promise* after we do one last inspection, we'll work on our science fair project," pleaded Beatrice. So Nora agreed.

Beatrice grabbed her spy backpack, and they snuck into the classroom to investigate. Nora stood watch.

"I don't understand," said Beatrice. "I just can't seem to find the source of the—"

They looked up.

"GOO!" they shouted.

"I need to get up there," said Beatrice.
"Can't . . . quite . . . reach. . . ."

"Hurry," said Nora. "Principal Louis
is coming!"

Beatrice scampered down just in time.

"Shouldn't you girls be outside?" asked Principal Louis.

"On our way!"

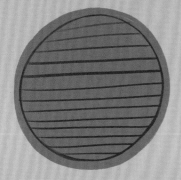

"We were so close!" said Beatrice.

"What if the roof is melting!"

"What if it's alien goo! If only there was a way to see into the ceiling. . . ."

"Could you look in the air vent from here?" Nora asked.

"Great thinking! I'll use my extendable Spy-o-scope!" Beatrice stretched. She did jumping jacks.

"What are you doing?" asked Nora.

"Exercising. Spies need to be nimble."

Beatrice climbed.

She balanced.

She positioned her Spy-o-scope in the vent.

"See anything?" asked Nora.
"No."

"Wait a minute . . ."

"BEEEEEES!" Beatrice shouted,
scrambling down.

"Know what else is sticky?" asked Beatrice.

"Honey! Which has sugar molecules. And we've already collected, analyzed, and compared our sample. Beatrice, do you know what this means?"

They looked at each other. "Our science fair project!"

"Lucky for us," said Nora, "there's a lot of science in spying."

Beatrice grinned. "Now, *that's* fair."

The next day, Miss Leland held class outside while the bee rescuers safely removed the hive.

"Why did the bees go in the ceiling?" said Lucy.

"What will happen to them now?" said Spencer.

"They'll be fine," the beekeeper explained. "Bees like dry, well-ventilated places, so the school air vent seemed like a perfect home to them. We have the queen, so once we introduce the bees to a new hive, they'll team up and get right back to work."

The next week, Nora and Beatrice's display was the buzz of the science fair.

"Honey *and* a first-place ribbon?" said Nora, giving Beatrice a high-five. "You're a pretty sweet spy, Beatrice."

"No," said Beatrice. "I'm a *super* spy. And you are one super partner."